This book belongs to:

_____

_____

_____

For Maisie, who we miss every day.

Published by  **KAMA** Publishing

19A The Swale, Norwich, NR5 9HE

www.kamapublishing.co.uk

Text © Kevin Price, 2012

Illustrations © Vicky Fieldhouse, 2012

British Library Cataloguing in Publishing Data.
A catalogue record for this book is available from the British Library.

ISBN 978-0-9567196-4-5

Printed in Great Britain by
Barnwell Print Ltd, Dunkirk, Aylsham, Norfolk. NR11 6SU

WORLD LAND TRUST™

www.carbonbalancedpaper.com
CBP0009851508120436

By using Carbon Balanced Paper
through the World Land Trust on this
publication we have saved 1077kg of
Carbon & preserved 90.47sqm of
critically threatened tropical forests.

Carbon Balanced Paper. One of the most sustainable forms of communication that
will reduce your carbon foot print and promote CSR. www.carbonbalancepaper.com

FUN AND GAMES AT THE ZOO

Kevin Price   Vicky Fieldhouse

Maisie and Bertie are down at the zoo,
Spending the day with the animal crew.

They're having a fabulous Fun Day today,
How many games do you think they can play?
Let's go and see, but before we begin,
Maisie says she would like you to join in.

Right, are you ready for game number one?
Who can run fastest? Now that should be fun!
Cheetah's the one who can run really fast,
If you race with him then you're bound to come last!

Maisie and Bertie say, "Run on the spot as fast as you can!"

Can you find and count 1 chipmunk?

Let's move along now to game number two,
Hopping and jumping with Red Kangaroo.
Her powerful legs help her jump really high,
It's brilliant fun, why don't you have a try?

Maisie & Bertie say,
"Jump as high as you can!"

Can you find and count 2 chipmunks?

Maisie and Bertie say, "Pretend to swing on the vines!"

Can you find and count 3 chipmunks?

What do you think could be game number three?
Swinging through trees with the young Chimpanzees.

The Chimpanzees' arms are incredibly strong,
So they'll show you tricks as you're swinging along.

Quick now, we're just starting game number four,
Let's see who can give out the mightiest roar!
The Lion's the noisiest cat in the zoo,
But I've heard that your roar is loud – is that true?

Maisie and Bertie say, "Do your loudest roar!"

Can you find and count 4 chipmunks?

It's time we were going to game number five,
We're off to the Penguin Pool, learning to dive.

Shut your eyes, pinch your nose and make a quick dash,
Then jump in the pool with a ginormous splash!

Maisie and Bertie say,
"Shut your eyes, pinch
your nose and jump!"

Can you find and count 5 chipmunks?

Maisie and Bertie say,
"Pull your funniest face!"

Can you find and count 6 chipmunks?

We're off to the forest for game number six,
We're helping the Monkeys to play naughty tricks.
We'll tweak Tiger's tail and we'll pull funny faces
And get up to mischief in all sorts of places.

Game number seven, are you ready for that?
Let's hang upside down with the giant Fruit Bats.
Well, that looks great fun and it's keeping you busy,
Don't do it for long or you'll start to feel dizzy!

Maisie and Bertie say, "Hang upside down if you can!"

Can you find and count 7 chipmunks?

Come on, hurry up, we're on game number eight,
We're riding an Elephant, please don't be late.
We'll sit on his back and then slide down his trunk;
Be careful, you might squash a little Chipmunk!

Maisie and Bertie say, "Slide down Mum or Dad's leg!"

Can you find and count 8 chipmunks?

Maisie and Bertie say,
"Roll on the ground!"

Can you find and count 9 chipmunks?

We're reaching the end; we're on game number nine,
We're rolling around with the young Porcupines.
This is a game that the Porcupines like,
But now that it's autumn, leaves stick to their spikes!

We've come to the finish, so have you had fun?
We hope you've enjoyed all the things that we've done. We've run with a Cheetah and jumped with a 'roo,

We've swung with the Chimpanzees over the zoo, we've roared with a Lion and dived in the pool,

Played tricks with the Monkeys (and wasn't that cool!), we've hung upside down with the beautiful Bats,

And ridden an Elephant! What about that! We've rolled on the ground with the young Porcupines,

And now we've arrived at the end of the line.

There's time for one more, let's play game number ten,
Curl up in your bed like a Bear in his den,
Close both your eyes and then start counting sheep,
And have some nice dreams when you drift off to sleep.

Bertie says, "It's time to sleep –
sweet dreams."

Can you find and count 10 chipmunks?

Help us to save Animals in the Wild

Animals in zoos are assured a good home,
But what of the ones who are destined to roam?
They live in the wild and face problems galore;
Their forests are taken and then, what is more,
They get into trouble for eating the crops
Of poor people who haven't got any shops.

Elephants in India and fierce tigers too
Need food to eat, just like the ones in the zoo.
World Land Trust buys land and then sets it aside
So they can roam freely and don't have to hide.
Reserves are protected by park guards and rangers
To make sure they're sheltered from all sorts of dangers.

Sir David Attenborough supports our Trust;
He thinks it's important and feels that we must
Save land for the animals while there's still time;
To lose them would be a most terrible crime.
While Bertie keeps animals safe in the zoo,
The future of wild ones rests with me and you.

By Viv Burton of the World Land Trust

WORLD
LAND
TRUST

The World Land Trust was established in 1989 to protect critically threatened habitats for their wildlife. So far over 500,000 acres have been saved throughout the world and are now protected by local organisations as nature reserves.

All donations resulting from the sale of this book will be used by World Land Trust's overseas project partners to fund park rangers who ensure that the reserves remain safe for animals in the wild.

World Land Trust is a registered charity No. 1001291. Its Patrons are Sir David Attenborough and David Gower.

A donation will save Real Acres in Real Places

For information or a School Pack please contact:
World Land Trust, Blyth House, Bridge Street,
Halesworth, Suffolk
IP19 8AB
Telephone: 01986 874 422

www.worldlandtrust.org

The End